Disney PRINCESS
Sleeping Beauty

Adapted by Mary Man-Kong

Illustrated by the Disney Storybook Art Team

Random House 🏠 New York

Dear Parents:

Congratulations! Your child is taking the first steps on an exciting journey. The destination? Independent reading!

STEP INTO READING® will help your child get there. The program offers five steps to reading success. Each step includes fun stories and colorful art or photographs. In addition to original fiction and books with favorite characters, there are Step into Reading Non-Fiction Readers, Phonics Readers and Boxed Sets, Sticker Readers, and Comic Readers—a complete literacy program with something to interest every child.

Learning to Read, Step by Step!

Ready to Read   Preschool–Kindergarten
• big type and easy words • rhyme and rhythm • picture clues
For children who know the alphabet and are eager to begin reading.

Reading with Help   Preschool–Grade 1
• basic vocabulary • short sentences • simple stories
For children who recognize familiar words and sound out new words with help.

Reading on Your Own   Grades 1–3
• engaging characters • easy-to-follow plots • popular topics
For children who are ready to read on their own.

Reading Paragraphs   Grades 2–3
• challenging vocabulary • short paragraphs • exciting stories
For newly independent readers who read simple sentences with confidence.

Ready for Chapters   Grades 2–4
• chapters • longer paragraphs • full-color art
For children who want to take the plunge into chapter books but still like colorful pictures.

STEP INTO READING® is designed to give every child a successful reading experience. The grade levels are only guides; children will progress through the steps at their own speed, developing confidence in their reading.

Remember, a lifetime love of reading starts with a single step!

For Annie and Margaret —M.M.-K.

Visit us on the Web!
StepIntoReading.com
randomhouse.com/kids

Educators and librarians, for a variety of teaching tools, visit us at RHTeachersLibrarians.com

ISBN 978-0-7364-3226-9 (trade) — ISBN 978-0-7364-8152-6 (lib. bdg.)
ISBN 978-0-7364-3225-2 (ebook)

Printed in the United States of America   10 9 8 7 6 5 4 3 2 1

Long ago,
a king and a queen
had a baby girl.
They named her Aurora.

The kingdom
had a party
for the new princess.
Three good fairies came.

Flora gave Aurora
the gift of beauty.

Fauna gave Aurora
the gift of song.

The witch Maleficent
came to the party.
She cast an evil spell.
The spell said that
on Aurora's sixteenth
birthday, she would
prick her finger
on a spinning wheel
and meet her end.

Luckily, the third good fairy, Merryweather, still had a gift to give.

She changed Maleficent's
spell so Aurora would fall
asleep when she pricked
her finger.

Only True Love's Kiss
would wake her.

Years passed.

The fairies hid Aurora

from Maleficent.

They called her

Briar Rose.

She did not know

she was a princess.

On Briar Rose's
sixteenth birthday,
the fairies wanted to
throw a surprise party.

They sent Briar Rose

to pick berries.

Briar Rose met a boy
named Phillip.
They fell in love.

The fairies used their magic
to get ready for the party.

Maleficent's bird
saw the magic!
He told Maleficent
he had found the fairies
and the princess!

Briar Rose loved
her cake and her new dress.
She told her aunts
she was in love.

The fairies told her
she was Princess Aurora.
She had to return to the
palace to marry a prince.

Aurora was very sad.
She wanted to be
with Phillip.

Back at the castle,
Maleficent made
a magical green ball.
Aurora followed it.

Aurora found
a spinning wheel.
"Touch it!"
Maleficent ordered.

Aurora obeyed.
She pricked her
finger and fell into
a deep sleep!
Maleficent cackled
and ran away.

The three fairies
found Aurora.
They took her
to a tower room.
They cast a spell.

The kingdom would
sleep until Aurora's true
love woke her with a kiss.

The fairies knew Phillip
loved Aurora.
They gave him
a magic sword.

Maleficent turned
into a dragon.
Phillip threw his
sword at her.
She was gone forever!

Phillip was the prince!
He found Aurora
and kissed her.

Aurora woke up.

The kingdom woke up.

The king and queen
were very happy.

Phillip and Aurora
danced and danced.
Everyone lived
happily ever after!